the
Flatulent
Pumpkin

an Improved Quality Self Published Enterprise

by Rodney Evans

First Steps Publishing

Tales of the Flatulent Pumpkin
Copyright © 2011 by Rodney Evans
© 2012 First Print Edition
CreateSpace

ISBN-13: 978-0983989059

www.LessonsInCharacter.com

Cover art by Gary Wein
Cover design by Suzanne Fyhrie Parrott
Book layout and design by First Steps Publishing

Printed in the United States of America

Dedicated to

Nellie Sue Walden,

Dr. Frankie Loving and

a wonderful creative team.

Learning never exhausts the mind.

~ Da Vinci

Wisdom begins in wonder.

~ Socrates

The time is always right to do the right thing.

~ King

Contents

IT WAS A BORING LITTLE TOWN stuck in the middle of almost nowhere. Nestled in a valley between a lake, a mountain, and a forest, the town of Darlinia was the perfect place to live if you wanted to have no fun. It was perfect for grown-ups. The town's children had given it three names. They called it plain, boring, and just plain boring. If it weren't for the excitement of Christmas and Halloween, there would almost never be anything fun to do.

Today is the beginning of change. A change that will cause all the townspeople to get so excited about each new day they'll spring out of bed each morning. Roosters will want to crow instead of viewing it as just a job. Tommy Shepard's mean ole dog will still greet everyone with a grunt or a growl, but on some days he might even smile.

Today is the day the orangey light burst through Jeremiah Johnson's bedroom window and changed everything. That orange light was the most magical thing to happen anywhere, and it happened in boring, little, Darlinia!

* * *

The Tale Begins...

It was the strangest of noises. The first time it awakened JJ he did what he always did, pulled the covers over his head and went back to his sleep. When the strange noise woke him a second time, his head popped up from beneath the covers. The sound had stopped but there was an orangey-yellow glare, not quite the color of the morning sun, coming through his curtains. Was he dreaming? Dreams do have a way of making themselves feel so real you might not know you were dreaming.

History tells us how JJ dealt with this mysterious light invading his slumber. He pulled the covers back over his head again, closed his eyes and snored.

Not what you would expect from a hero.

A few moments passed and then, in the middle of one of his snores, JJ sprang completely upright. There he sat, motionless and thinking. Winter was so cold there had been no sunshine in weeks, and it wasn't yet time for the sun to rise! What on earth was glowing outside of his window? Curiously, he peeked through his curtains to find an orange light shining from the direction of town.

His house was so warm he really hated to walk into the frigid winter, but he had to find out about that strange light. Before

braving the cold, JJ wrapped himself in so many clothes his mom would be proud. The orange light was easy to follow because it lit up the sky. On his tenth step JJ noticed that the light began to fade. It was such a peculiar thing. Each step he took, the light grew dimmer. Having to hurry before it went away altogether JJ broke into a run, going as fast as he could with all those clothes on. But, by the time he turned the last corner, the light was completely gone! He looked all over trying to find where the light had come from but there was nothing orange there except the little thing he'd planted, watered and fed for the past six months. No longer a little thing, it was now standing **five feet** tall!

Losing track of time, JJ wasn't sure how long he'd been staring at the huge pumpkin when his best friends, Ronnie, Matt and Suzy, came along. They too had seen the orange sky and, dressed in their floppiest clothes, came to check things out.

"JJ, what happened to your pumpkin?!" asked Suzy.

"I don't know," said JJ. "I heard a noise and saw the sky glowing. The light went out before I got here. Then I saw this!" he said, pointing his finger to the gigantic pumpkin. They asked him what was making the orange light, so JJ told them it must have been the pumpkin but the light had vanished before he could see for sure.

It was too early and too cold for any of them to be outside and, to be honest, the big pumpkin scared them. After talking for a few minutes, they agreed not to tell anyone and the others went back home. JJ stayed behind a little longer.

He sat on the ground, leaning his back against the pumpkin. Looking down the road, a peculiar little thing caught his eye. There are those who would later say that it was even more surprising than the big pumpkin. Nothing grew there at the Farley home; not one

flower, not one shrub . . . not even grass! But right now JJ swore he saw a pretty red flower growing on the left side of the Farley home. How strange.

While walking home JJ heard a long rumbling sound somewhere behind him.

"FFBBTTTT."

It was loud and disturbing, but at least now he knew where the sound that had awakened him came from. He thought it was the combined sound of seventeen cows farting at the same moment. Everyone knew that one deadly cow fart could get lodged in your brain and mess up your whole day. Our hero broke into a run and made it home faster than ever. Little did he know cows had nothing to do with the mysterious sound.

The rooster crowed to begin the day and houses started coming to life. Moms cooked the best breakfasts. Dads left for work. Children finished their morning chores. With no school that day, due to the extremely cold winter, they had nothing to do except bore themselves silly again. Tommy Shepard sat in his room playing with the same toy cars. Freckle-faced Angel dressed the same three dolls for the twenty-ninth time in two days. Jenny Raisen curled by the fireplace reading yet another book on hair care. Unless you were an adult, there were only so many times you could read the same book, dress the same dolls and play the same games before becoming so bored you might toot just for the fun of it.

Sometime in the early afternoon the town bell rang three times. Everyone stopped what they were doing and headed to the town square. They were shocked at the sight of a pumpkin that was almost five feet tall! Even more shocking than seeing the giant

pumpkin was seeing a living plant at the Farley place. Ms. Jenkins was so shocked she almost fainted twice.

A very unhappy Mayor walked into the square and began to speak. "It breaks my heart to tell you such bad news."

A squeaky sound from behind him interrupted his speech. The children ignored what sounded like another Mayor-cuts-the-cheese moment. The Mayor began again, "Like I was saying . . . it breaks my heart to tell you this, but it's very important that I say . . ."

"PPFFBBBBBbbbbbtttttttrrrrrrTTTT!!!"

The sound was so close and so loud it startled the Mayor, making him jump to his tippy toes for a second.

"Ha! Ha!" people giggled.

A very flustered Mayor held his head high and tried to continue, but he had now forgotten what he was about to say. After a short pause to collect his thoughts he continued, "There will be no school again tomorrow. It's going to get much colder. Everyone should stay inside and make sure you have plenty of firewood, food and games. Today we should let the children outside to play because tomorrow will be too cold."

Finally the Mayor took full notice of the pumpkin behind him. He beamed a bright smile while congratulating JJ on how large it had grown. Reaching over to pat the pumpkin, he felt the ground rumble followed by a very soft,

"bbbbrrruuummmPPP."

Looking around quickly he asked, "Did anyone feel that?"

Adults stared at the Mayor, giving him their most disapproving looks. Although his hearing wasn't what it used to be, the Mayor knew a fart when he heard one.

He said, "I know somebody, besides me, must have heard the ground shake." The Mayor was the only one near the pumpkin though, so he didn't realize he was the only person who had felt anything.

"We heard you loud and clear," said Mabel Farley sternly.

Trying to change the subject the Mayor said, "Mabel, what lovely plants in your yard. You simply must tell us the special thing you did to ..."

"PPPBBBBBTTTTTPop.Pop.POP!"

His question was cut off by a long honking expulsion of air ending in a series of soft pops. Mabel Farley glared at the Mayor so hard he almost ran away. He muttered something about urgent business, and walked away so fast he was nearly running.

Several children could no longer contain themselves and were now rolling on the ground in fits of giggles. Others were busy mimicking the giant fart they heard. The Mayor was known for farting the big fart.

Mabel Farley was such a nice lady, she didn't deserve to be ridiculed or made to suffer through another of the Mayor's gigantic farts. It wasn't her fault that her cooking never tasted right. Nor was it her fault that plants refused to stay alive in her yard.

The Sheriff stepped forward and repeated the Mayor's message.

"The Mayor has some urgent business to attend to. Your children have been spending a lot of time inside because of the cold. Send them outside today because it will be too cold to play outdoors in the coming days."

Then the Sheriff left to check on the Mayor. It had been a huge fart and the Sheriff needed to see how his best friend was handling it.

The children played in the snow and had the time of their lives. They loved it so! They broke out all their sleds and made the best snowmen. Moms smiled to see them so happy and brought them a steady supply of steamy hot chocolate.

JJ, Ronnie, Matt and Suzy huddled by the pumpkin and agreed to keep their secret about seeing that weird orange light. Everyone congratulated JJ on the marvelous size of his pumpkin. Many of the children had planted things in the town park in the spring. There were flowers, fruit trees and just about everything else. Suzy had planted an entire row of red flowers. Ronnie had planted what he thought were magic beans. JJ had planted a pumpkin but was the only kid in town who watered and fed his plant every day.

That night at dinner JJ almost told his parents about the orange light. But instead of telling them he fell asleep, dropping his head into his bowl of chicken soup with a splash.

"Poor baby. He played his little heart out today," said his mom.

His father lifted JJ's head out of the soup, cleaned his curly souped hair and quietly put him to bed.

Several days passed and the weather did exactly as the Mayor had predicted — it turned much colder. Inside each home was the same old story; children played the same games, dressed the same dolls, and read the same books.

JJ didn't have an answer for the mysterious orange light so he focused on trying to figure out how the pumpkin got so tall so quick. When he couldn't come up with any decent answers, he focused on trying to figure out what that strange noise was that awakened him and that had erupted behind him that morning. His answer was cows, because there was no way a sound of any kind had anything to do with a pumpkin.

Early one morning JJ was again awakened by a strange noise and another glowing orange light, which was even brighter. Again he threw on all the floppy clothes he could, and bravely trudged into the middle of that horribly freezing morning.

The orange light led him back to the town square. This time when he turned the last corner he nearly jumped out of his skin. Standing before him the pumpkin was nearly as tall as a tree; it had doubled in size since the last time he saw it! And it was the source of that wonderful light. JJ had to know what a glowing pumpkin felt like, so he walked over and placed his hands flat against it. His fingertips and palms touched peach fuzz. It wasn't hot, but it was warm. On this frigid cold morning being near the pumpkin was as warm as being at home.

JJ braced his back against it and eased himself into a comfortable sitting position. Winter was so cold he started thinking how much he missed warm weather. His mind transported him to memories of sunny days when he and the other kids were playing in the square and planting the garden. He wanted to be able to play outside for hours and not worry about floppy clothes.

"That thing's a monster!" Ronnie called loudly as he turned the corner.

"I don't know how it happened," replied JJ, still sitting with his back against the big orange pumpkin.

A little later Matt and Suzy turned up the street, both wrapped from head to toe and looking like young zombies. An astonished Suzy couldn't believe her own eyes. She was having a hard time accepting the giant pumpkin as the same one JJ planted.

"Someone must have pumped air into it!" she exclaimed.

"I don't see how, but it's frigid cold out here and this pumpkin is warm enough to heat my house. Come touch it, Suzy," said JJ, standing up.

A scared Suzy had only taken one slow step towards JJ when a soft gush of air sounded from the pumpkin and ended in a squishy,

"Pop."

JJ vanished.

The horrified trio froze, staring at the spot where JJ had just been standing. The first to bolt was Suzy. The boys felt someone had to be brave and wait for their friend. They lasted all of three seconds before they both took off running.

Zombies don't run very fast and fall over quite often. Ronnie managed to fall only twice before making it home. All those clothes made it extremely difficult to get back up. So he stopped trying to run so fast. In the end he made it home by shuffling as fast as he could without falling. It made him look like a real zombie.

* * *

"Where am I?" JJ said to no one in particular.

Except for the near blackness surrounding him, JJ couldn't see much. He stood wondering where he was and where his friends had gone. His ears told him there was some whooshing going on in the distance, but there was no way to tell what was making the sound. A moment ago he had been standing by the pumpkin feeling pleasantly warm. Now it was so hot sweat was beginning to pour from his forehead.

He didn't care where he was. Nor did he care that it was nearly too dark to see. He just knew it was much too warm to wear two

coats. Off came his gloves. Off came the polka dot scarf his mom made him wear. Off came the two coats, and yet he was still too hot. Next to come off was the purple sweater his grandmother had given him last year. Then he removed the brown sweater she had given him the year before that. Then off came the flannel shirt from his dad. By now the mass of clothes lying before him was nearly as high as his knees.

JJ was down to his floppy underwear and his very special t-shirt, looking like he was about to turn in for bed. However, he was still wearing his droopy boots and a ball cap. Wishing he had a little more light, he tentatively stepped forward. Before finishing his second step he thought he heard a baby innocently passing a cute little toot! He looked around but, of course, there was no baby.

Suddenly, a marble-sized ball of shining rainbow lights appeared and headed straight for him. The spinning ball of light stopped before his face, remaining suspended just beyond his nose. Its brilliant yellow, orange, red and green was quite pretty. The swirling rainbow light brightened as it moved higher, out of JJ's reach. The further the ball moved up and away the more it expanded and the brighter it became. Before long it had traveled into the distance and had grown into a large ball that resembled a swirling rainbow-colored sun. It was now bright enough for JJ to make out green grass, trees, flowers and a lake.

There was no way his eyes were working correctly. So he closed them for a moment. When he opened them again, he found himself looking at a beautiful summer day. He saw a large tree with strong branches, deep green leaves and enormous yellow flowers. The sky was bright. Luscious green grass flowed everywhere, scattered with colorful flowers. The bluest blue sky was a perfect

backdrop for the pretty scenery which stretched all around him. That was when he realized how alone he was.

* * *

"Honey," said Mrs. Johnson to her husband, "there is a knock at the door."

JJ's father hurried downstairs to find the Sheriff waiting patiently. The Sheriff told him the strange story he had heard about JJ disappearing. The Sheriff said it was probably just another joke the kids thought was funny. Understandably worried about their son, Mr. and Mrs. Johnson went with the Sheriff to the last place he had been seen. Several townspeople had also heard the story and they all gathered around the pumpkin. Because he was respectful, hard working, smart and always tried to do the right thing, JJ was well-liked. The worst thing anyone ever said about him was, as a big practical joker, sometimes his jokes got out of control.

The crowd gathering near the pumpkin was treated to the weirdest sounds they had ever heard. The pumpkin was belting out gushes of wind, splats, belches and other strange noises. So terrified were several adults, they tried to hide behind their children! The children, who had been bored silly up until now, showed not one ounce of fear and handled the situation as children normally do — they giggled.

Maybe they understood that flatulence should never be taken too seriously. It has two main purposes which are to make you feel better and to make you giggle. This was proof positive that kids preferred a cold day of flatulence to another warm day of being bored, bored, bored.

Jenny Raisen had to raise her voice over the loud sounds of the pumpkin's concert of flatulence.

"It's just a pumpkin," she said. "There's no such thing as a bad one. JJ planted and took care of it. It hasn't been mean or scary."

Standing only half as tall as the pumpkin, these were brave words coming from a ten-year-old girl, and she was right.

Somehow the Sheriff's arrival, along with Mr. & Mrs. Johnson, had a calming effect on the crowd and the pumpkin, and quiet settled over town square. A shocked Mrs. Johnson nearly fainted upon laying eyes on the pumpkin. She remembered it being big, but now, she thought, it's a giant!

"I'm forming a search party," announced the Sheriff. "JJ is playing a joke on us all and has to be hiding somewhere. First he turns a cute little pumpkin into this," he said, pointing at the big pumpkin, "then he runs and hides. Who wants to join the search party?"

The Sheriff told Suzy, Matt and Ronnie, who were with JJ when he disappeared, that each would lead a search team to where they thought he might be hiding. JJ's friends tried their best to convince the Sheriff that this was no joke; they had each seen JJ disappear when the pumpkin pooted.

The Sheriff would have none of it.

"People poot. Pumpkins don't. It's just another of JJ's tricks."

"It's no trick," said Mr. Johnson.

"I'll show you it's a trick," the Sheriff declared.

He placed both hands on the pumpkin and pushed. When he pushed he felt a soft rumble. Then he screamed and ran a few steps before realizing the scream he heard was his and that everyone was looking.

"It's dangerous!" he screamed again.

The sight of a big terrified man was priceless.

"Nothing my son does is dangerous. I'll show you," exclaimed Mrs. Johnson as she positioned herself exactly where the Sheriff had been during his first scream.

"Stop! It's dangerous!" repeated the Sheriff.

Mrs. Johnson didn't hesitate for a moment. "If my son planted and watered this plant every day, then it's not dangerous to anyone," she insisted.

Somehow her hands touched the exact same place on the pumpkin as JJ's had earlier. She felt a warm peach fuzz sensation and smiled, her grin one of enormous pride. Moments later the pumpkin emitted a soft gust of wind followed by a good sized farting sound ending in the same,

"Pop!"

And there was JJ.

It wasn't the first time he had been in front of everyone, but it was the first time he stood before them in the freezing cold wearing floppy underwear and his "Mommy's Special Son" t-shirt. Mrs. Johnson let out a scream and fainted. The Sheriff fainted too and hit the ground before she did.

JJ was more worried about his mom than being seen in his underwear. He knelt at her side.

"Mom!" he shouted, "Are you all right?"

"She is going to be fine, son, now that she knows you are fine," his dad reassured him. "JJ, put your clothes back on before she awakens. If she sees you in your underwear in public she will faint again."

"Oh, yeah, my clothes. I wonder where they are?" He stood up and looked at the crowd. "Has anyone seen my clothes?" he asked.

The crowd giggled.

"No, silly," someone said. "They are probably wherever you left them."

JJ thought hard for a minute then said, "That's the problem. I don't know where I was."

"Does that shirt mean what I think it means?" asked his best friend Ronnie.

Looking down at his chest JJ finally understood why they were laughing. Thinking really hard he still couldn't figure out where he had been, but he did remember green grass, pretty flowers, a nice lake and a bright swirling sun. Before he could tell everyone what he had seen, he realized that the cold was quickly overtaking him. In a few more minutes it would creep right into his bones.

Upon his arrival the first two things the Mayor saw were JJ in his underwear and the galactic-sized pumpkin and he knew he was losing his mind. He somehow managed to remain calm and walked over to rouse the Sheriff.

JJ was so cold he wished for his clothes with all his might. Just as his mind released this thought a soft breeze arose from nowhere. Accompanying it was a squeezing sound, kinda long, ending in a squishy,

"PPPFFFBBTT."

All eyes went to the Mayor.

"I didn't do that!" he insisted.

"It's raining something!" someone yelled.

Drifting from the sky were objects of different colors, but

these didn't fall straight down like rain. They were JJ's clothes, drifting downward in a slow rocking motion, side to side, like watching a playground swing!

Shocked and mesmerized the Sheriff screamed, "I told you it was a trick! How did you do that?"

"It's no trick, Sheriff. I didn't do anything except wish for my clothes," JJ answered.

Something clicked in JJ's mind and this was the very moment that changed everything. He was about to place his hands on the pumpkin when the Sheriff shouted,

"Don't touch that thing! It's dangerous."

JJ hesitated. He thought of the orangey glow and farting noises. He remembered what had happened after he wished for light and what had happened after he wished for his clothes. Light and clothes were little things, but they were things that he had wished for. And these weren't large wishes; they were more like just saying, I wish.

Now he was thinking about deliberately wishing for something. If it happened, it would be big and it would be for everyone. Concentrating very hard he placed his hands on the pumpkin and wished. But he quickly began to feel silly when nothing happened. However, moments later the bottom of the giant pumpkin emitted that same orange glow which rose until it completely covered the pumpkin.

There was a rumble, then a large rush of wind. The pumpkin wobbled just a little as it emitted an audible,

"PPPbbbbbBBBBBBTTTTT."

It started as a squeaky one and continued on and on getting louder and louder! People began either laughing or running. The

Minister, standing in the crowd, burst into uncontrollable giggles. He said to himself that it sounded like someone was trying to poot his brains out. The Mayor looked for the Sheriff to tell him to do something, but the Sheriff had run away and was nowhere to be found.

Abruptly, the farting stopped.

Then the pumpkin let out another of its surprises. It hissed and engulfed itself in a fog. A red, yellow and blue fog, which looked rather like a rainbow. It began swirling around the pumpkin. It was such a strange sight no one moved. Even Tommy Shepard's dog stopped barking.

That foggy rainbow started spinning faster and rising until it was hovering over the pumpkin. Then it ascended into the sky, all the while growing larger and larger. Minutes later the sky was filled with a rainbow of colors swirling in a sphere that looked almost like the sun and, best of all, giving off heat just like the sun!

Off came everyone's huge winter coats. Out came people from their homes, who had been hiding from the cold. With the rainbow colors raining down on the entire town, JJ's mom, who had woken from her faint, finally got a perfectly good look at JJ in his underwear.

The poor lady fainted again.

Returning from wherever he had been hiding, the Sheriff sternly told JJ, "Get that thing down. It'll fall out of the sky and hurt someone! There is no telling just how much damage a thing like that can do."

He looked around and noticed everyone taking off their coats. Patches of ice were melting for the first time in months. Flowers bloomed before his eyes and grass turned green. The kids were

starting to run around like little kids should. For the first time in a long time, sweat ran down the Sheriff's face.

JJ's dad walked up to the Sheriff and said,

"I'll be the first to help you get the rainbow down if you can tell me how. That swirly thing up there might not be the sun but it sure feels right. Children are supposed to play like that. And tomorrow I am going do something I've wanted to do for quite some time. I'm going fishing!"

No one understood what had just happened. They only knew they could feel heat from the swirly thing. They knew the swirly thing came from JJ's pumpkin, and they knew JJ had made it happen while wearing his underwear.

The Mayor was finding it difficult trying to cope.

"I am the Mayor of a town where a huge pumpkin farted a rainbow. It might just be the most fantastic poot in history!"

Darlinia is forever tucked in the middle of almost nowhere, but the fun is just beginning. Every day is a promise full of magical wishes from the greatest gift of all, the magic of flatulence. It's the gift that keeps on giving.

The End

A word from the Author

The creative origins of the Flatulent Pumpkin stories

"I make up stories instantly, and even I don't know when a story will emerge. This one happened at the family dinner table when the words "Flatulent Pumpkin" left my lips in complete surprise to me. I was so shocked by my family's hysterical laughter, I made up a story about a pumpkin dispensing wisdom in the center of town.

To make it interesting I added magic. But the pumpkin didn't have perfect control of its magic. No one would never know, not even the pumpkin, when "pumpkin magic" might happen. The pumpkin would smile sheepishly whenever it was surprised by its own magic and/or its own flatulence.

Most of the Flatulent Pumpkin's creative elements began that night, when, for thirty minutes, I cracked the family up with the story of a flatulent and magical vegetable.

This time the family said to me, "You have to write that one down!"

~ Rodney Evans"

More Flatulent Pumpkin Tales

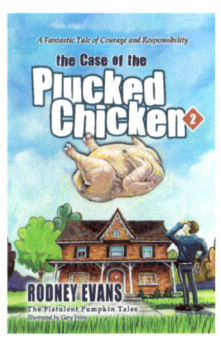

The Case of the Plucked Chicken #2

Lesson in Courage and Responsibility
In this second Flatulent Pumpkin tale, a mysterious appearance surprises the small town of Darlinia and wrecks havoc. The town sheriff is determined to close the case and return everything to normal. See if you can solve *The Case of the Plucked Chicken* before the sheriff.

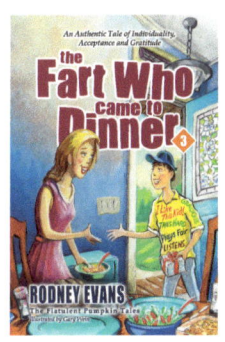

The Fart Who Came to Dinner #3

Lessons in Consideration
The third in the *Tales of the Flatulent Pumpkin* series breaks new ground in laughter and acceptance. You won't be able to stop laughing when the new kid comes to town.

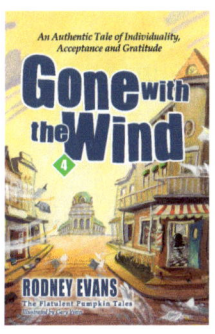

Gone With the Wind #4

Lessons in Determination, Responsibility and Family
A girl's determination surprisingly gives the town its most magical moments ever. Her wish transforms the town and provides the greatest lesson of all time.

About the Author

Born on September 11, Rodney Evans was later called to active military service due to the events of 9/11.

He discovered his humorous writing ability by accident, many years ago. While reading a high school assignment out loud, the entire class and teacher surprised him by laughing hysterically. This happened again in college while reciting another writing assignment in which he created a character he titled *"Little Ugly"*.

Neither of these assignments was intended to be funny.

A native of Gulfport, MS, Rodney now resides in Winchester, VA, with his wife, children and dog, Buddy.

* * *

Enjoy more of Rodney's Tales of the Flatulent Pumpkin by reading *Case of the Plucked Chicken*, *The Fart Who Came to Dinner* and *Gone With the Wind*.

You can visit Rodney's website and blog at **LessonsInCharacter.com**.

www.ingramcontent.com/pod-product-compliance
Lightning Source LLC
Chambersburg PA
CBHW040859120626
46551CB00001B/87